For Virginia Alexander

Acknowledgments

Virginia Alexander, Jennifer Alison, Andrea Beeman, Emily Brooks, Jason Burch,
Christine Burgin, Ariel Dill, Matt Ducklo, Catherine Ecclestone, Ken Geist, Hyperion,
Mort Janklow, Marlo Kovach, Marian Maloney, Erick Michaud, Heather Murray,
Patrick O'Rourke, Dale Rubin, Katleen Sterck, Gary Tooth/Empire Design Studio,
and Pam Wegman

With special thanks to Mr. and Mrs. Samuel C.J. Spivey

Hands: Jason Burch, Matt Ducklo, Heather Murray
Dogs: Batty, Chip, Chundo

For information address Hyperion Books for Children,
114 Fifth Avenue, New York, New York 10011-5690.

Printed in Singapore
1 3 5 7 9 10 8 6 4 2

Design by Empire Design Studio, NYC
This book is set in Century Schoolbook, Trade Gothic, and Bureau Grotesque.
Library of Congress Cataloging-in-Publication Data on file.
ISBN 0-7868-0606-0

Visit www.hyperionchildrensbooks.com

ChipwantsaDog

William Wegman

To Mom
Happy B-day
love Sandi & Chelsea

Hyperion Books for Children
NEW YORK

2003

Dogs! Dogs! Dogs! Dogs!

All Chip ever thought about was dogs.

All he ever read about was dogs.

His room was a dog theme park.

Chip wondered, "If I had a dog, what would I name it?
Fido? Rover? Chundo?"

Even as a baby, Chip had wanted a dog.
"Dog" was his first word.

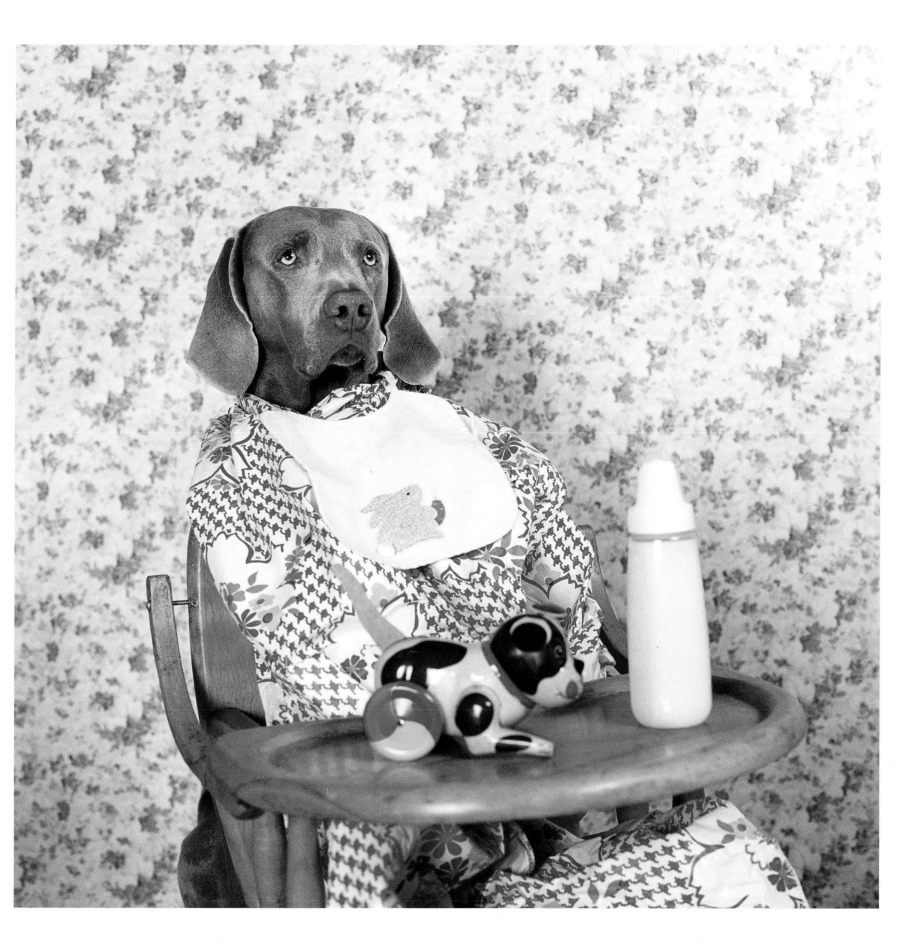

Without a dog, Chip was lonely.

"If only I had a dog…
I would have someone to play with."

"If I had a dog, I would teach it to do tricks."

"Rover, sit."

"Fido, stay."   "Chundo, fetch."

"Roll over, Fido, Rover, Chundo, or whoever you are."

"Good dog."

"If I had a dog, it would be my best friend."

But... Chip's parents DID NOT want a dog.

His mother liked cats.
She was a cat person.

"Dogs shed," she said.

"Dogs are a lot of responsibility," his father added.

"You wouldn't have time for your chores."

"There is nothing more to discuss."

"Why can't I have a dog?" asked Chip.

"All the other kids have dogs. *Tilly Madison* has a dog."

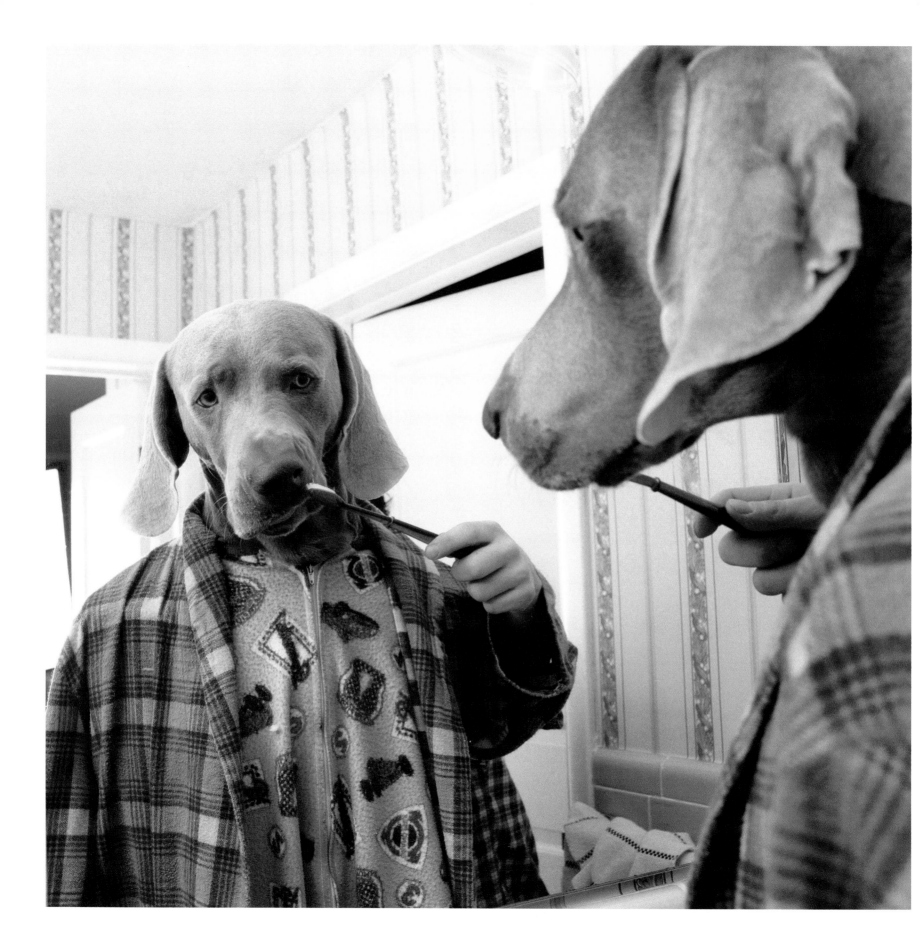

Before bedtime, Chip brushed his teeth.

He looked into the mirror for a long, long time.

"Why do I only think about dogs?" he wondered.

That night he had a dream....

In his dream he was a dog.

"I'm a dog!...I'm a dog!...I'm a dog!"

When Chip woke up...

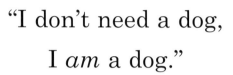

"I don't need a dog,
I *am* a dog."

That day, Chip began his new life.

He took himself for a walk, taught himself new tricks,
and gave himself a bone. He made many new friends
and was never lonely again.